WHAT JAMIE SAW

OTHER BOOKS BY CAROLYN COMAN

Tell Me Everything

what jamie saw

CAROLYN COMAN

FRONT STREET
ARDEN, NORTH CAROLINA
1995

For Susan and Sean Paradis,
with love and thanks

Copyright © 1995 by Carolyn Coman
Printed in the United States
Designed by Virginia Evans

Library of Congress Cataloging-in-Publication Data
Coman, Carolyn.
What Jamie saw / Carolyn Coman. — 1st ed.
p. cm.
Summary: Having fled to a family friend's hillside
trailer after his mother's boyfriend tried to throw his
baby sister against a wall, nine-year-old Jamie finds
himself living an existence full of
uncertainty and fear.
ISBN 1-886910-02-2
[1. Child abuse — Fiction.] I. Title.
PZ7.C729Wh 1995
[Fic] — dc20   95-23545

WHAT JAMIE SAW

Wʜᴇɴ Jᴀᴍɪᴇ sᴀᴡ ʜɪᴍ ᴛʜʀᴏᴡ ᴛʜᴇ baby, saw Van throw the little baby, saw Van throw his little sister Nin, when Jamie saw Van throw his baby sister Nin, then they moved. That very night—or was it early morning?—some time of day or night that felt like it had no hour at all, Jamie and his mother and Nin left the house where they'd been living with Van—Van's house—and they drove to Earl's apartment above Daggert's Sand 'n Gravel in Stark, New Hampshire, and from there they went on to the trailer.

Up until the second he saw Van throw the baby, Jamie had been sleeping, in the bedroom he shared with his half-sister, Nin. The sound of her crying and crying — she was such a crybaby — had gone inside Jamie's dream. In his dream the crying was some sort of siren or alarm. Was it a fire drill at school? Jamie was in his third-grade classroom with Mrs. Desrochers, and he was running around, even though he knew better, knew that he was supposed to walk, not run, and he was trying to figure out what to do.

It wasn't the crying that woke him up. It was some other sound — what was it? — something else that made him spring up in bed, lean back on his elbows, and open his eyes wide, just in time to see Van reach into the crib and grab Nin and throw her, fire her across the room, like a missile, like a bullet, like a shooting star, like a football.

No: like nothing Jamie'd ever seen before.

And quicker than Jamie could even take in what he'd just seen, quicker than any beginning or middle could possibly be, he saw the ending: saw his mother catch her, catch his baby sister Nin—there, plop, in her arms. Saw his mother step out of the dark hallway and into the lighted bedroom and raise up her arms, as if she'd been waiting her whole life to appear at that moment, exactly in that place, to raise up her arms and catch her flying baby.

Everything was dead quiet then. Jamie remembered: dead quiet, and heartbeats later Nin's delayed squall, and his mother crying "Oh my God," and finally her voice calling to him, saying, "Okay now, Jamie, I want you to get up and walk over here to me. Right over here to where I am standing. It's okay, you just get up out of your bed and walk right over here and nothing's going to happen. You just come over here to me."

She kept saying that, that lullaby, calling to Jamie, but he was still in bed, eyes wide, watching, and his body was frozen. "It's okay," he heard his mother saying, but it was like Nin's crying escaping into his dream. "It's okay now, Jamie-boy, you come over here to me."

Only his eyes could move, so Jamie moved them to look at Van, who was standing by Nin's crib. He was hanging his head. Everything about him was hanging: his shoulders hung and his arms hung from his shoulders, and his big hands hung off his arms. Hanging, drained. A big, dumb, drained bathtub.

"Come on now, honey. Come over here to me, climb out of that bed, and come over here to me and no one's going to hurt you."

Van was done. He wasn't going to hurt anybody, he was hanging his head. Jamie moved his eyes back to his mother and she was holding Nin tight against her and her words were slow and deliberate and powerful. "Come here by me, Jamie-boy."

Jamie lifted back the covers and his legs wouldn't move. He made them move, though, off the mattress and onto the floor and then he was sitting on the side of his bed. He looked at Van again. Van was still hanging, drained, done. And then Jamie bolted off his bed and shot across the room to his mother as fast and as straight as if Van had thrown him. He plowed into his mother and wrapped his arms around her waist. She put one hand against his back. Nin's little feet were close to the top of his head. And then the three of them, all attached, touching, a unit, shuffled back across the threshold and into the hallway.

Jamie's mother reached back and discon-
nected Jamie's grasp and then bent down
and very close to his face whispered fast,
"Good boy, Jamie, it's okay. We're okay.
You just do what I say now. We're going in
the car. You just do what I say."

She led him down the hallway and out
the front door, onto the cement steps.
Frigid winter air encased them. Jamie felt
the shock of it across his bare feet, felt the
pebbled flatness of the cement and the
mystery of standing outside in his long-
underwear pajamas at whatever hour of day
or night it was. The moment felt more
wonderful than terrible, because the terrible part was inside everything that was
happening but hadn't had time to catch up
and bloom yet, and Van was done, his head
was hanging, and his mother had caught
the baby and the night air was shocking
and clean.

His mother moved them quickly down the steps and across the frozen, snowless lawn, still holding Nin against her, and brought them to their big, rusty Buick in the driveway. She dropped Jamie's hand to yank open the door and told him, "Get in and wait right here and don't move."

Jamie climbed into the back seat next to the window, and his mother walked around to the other side, opened the door, and strapped Nin into her car seat. "I'll be right back," she said. "You hear me?" Jamie nodded.

Then she closed the door, clunk, and Jamie was alone with Nin in the dark car. His feet were frozen. He was shaking. He leaned across the seat to look at Nin. She looked the same. She didn't look hurt. She didn't look like she'd gone flying, like she'd been shot out of some cannon across the room.

Jamie turned and watched his mother step onto the lighted steps and go back into the house through the front door. He stopped breathing. He didn't breathe, and then she came out again, loaded down with blankets and pillows, clutching a mound of them to her. She crossed the lawn, opened the door next to Jamie, and began shoving the blankets and pillows inside. Jamie felt like he was getting packed somehow — wrapped up like a fragile, breakable object that his mother was taking hurried care to protect. She stuffed a comforter on the floor, and it dried the soles of his feet and sent the first wave of warmth through his body. "I'll be right back," she repeated, and once again shut the door.

One more time Jamie watched his mother go back into the house. He pictured her walking down the hallway, to the closet where she kept the sheets and blankets and winter coats. It was hard, though, to keep her moving, gathering what she was after to take with them, at the same time that Jamie (in his mind) held Van perfectly still, motionless, by the crib. It was like keeping one eye perfectly open and the other one shut. Even though Jamie was working hard at it, Van slipped in a movement—Jamie pictured him raising a hand, but it was just to rest it on the bar of Nin's crib, for extra support, for balance. He wasn't going to hurt anyone. He was done with that.

His mother appeared in the doorway again, alone, holding coats this time and pinching boots in her fingers. She deposited those in the trunk, tapped on the window next to Jamie's face, and went back inside.

For the third time Jamie held his breath and waited. When his mother came back out, she was clutching a pillowcase gathered at the neck, and Jamie saw the top of his baseball bat sticking out. She had collected a bag of toys. And even though Jamie knew it was his mother standing on Van's porch in the middle of the night, even though Van had thrown the baby, even though he didn't believe anymore, Jamie looked at his mother clutching the sack of toys and all he could think of was Santa Claus.

2

"DID YOU BRING MY MAGIC?" JAMIE
had been close to falling asleep in the back
seat. His mother had shifted the car into
reverse with a decisive, deep-bellied thunk
that Jamie felt in his bones, and had
backed out the driveway and headed off.
Jamie was warm finally, surrounded by all
the stuff she had packed around him, the
car heater blasting, and before they'd gone
very far at all, he was drifting off to sleep,
dreams sneaking up on him without his
even knowing, when suddenly he spoke,
and with a real urgency, too: "Did you
bring my magic?"

"Yes," his mother answered him right away. "It's in the bag." How quickly her one word stopped the ferocious pounding in his heart. She had put the magic book and tricks in the bag; she had caught the baby; they were on their way to Earl's—his mother said so, when she finally got in the car—and Jamie once again drifted off toward sleep.

He must've slept, because they arrived at Earl's place in Stark impossibly soon, as if Earl lived next door to Van, which he didn't. It was the gravel of Earl's U-turn driveway crunching under the tires that jostled Jamie awake again—waking up, back to sleep, waking, sleeping, the whole night long, it felt like—and his mother saying, "I hope he hasn't got other company." Nin kept on sleeping, even when Jamie's mother picked her up out of her car seat and they climbed the steps to Earl's apartment. Now that it didn't matter, Jamie thought, now that it was all right for her to cry her head off, there wasn't a peep out of her.

Jamie was holding a pillow, and his mother was holding Nin and a blanket and her purse. She knocked a good, solid knock on Earl's door, and they waited. After a little while she knocked again and they heard him rustling around inside, coming toward the door.

Just who did Jamie think was going to open that door? Earl, he knew. He knew that it was Earl who was coming. He knew that. But who was Earl? A lot of the time Jamie thought, or at least hoped, that Earl was his father. His mother had told him flat out that he wasn't, that Earl was not Jamie's father, he was her best friend—they'd been babies together—but plenty of times that made no difference. He liked Earl and he liked the idea that Earl was his father. Sometimes he thought that Earl was his mother's brother, which would have made Earl his uncle, and that would have been fine, too. For the most part, Earl was just Earl.

And that's who opened the door: just Earl, fresh out of bed, with his hair frizzled and sticking up in the back, his blue jeans pulled on and zipped but not snapped around his waist, and no shirt. "What?" he called out when he was close to the door, and then again, "What?" when he opened it, but the second time, when he saw who it was, that it was Patty, his "what" turned scared.

"S'okay," Patty said. She put her hand up as if she were stopping traffic. "We're just here." Jamie didn't think that explained much, but it seemed to do something for Earl, who didn't ask anything else, just told them to come on in. "I'll put on coffee," he said, and Patty nodded and said, "Let me get the kids down first."

It was definitely on the morning side of night now, more light than it was dark. And Jamie wasn't sure about going back to sleep again. Hadn't the day started once and for all? And weren't they at Earl's? He didn't sleep at Earl's. He watched TV there, in the big chair, and drank Cokes and ate cheese doodles, or he went outside with Earl and handed him tools when Earl was working on trucks or bucket loaders or caterpillars, or he practiced his magic tricks at the kitchen table, but he didn't sleep at Earl's.

His mother headed straight toward the pullout couch, though, in Earl's tiny living room right off the kitchen. She carefully set Nin down on the La-Z-Boy, and then tossed the cushions off the couch and yanked out the mattress. The bed squeaked a lot and the mattress was thin and seemed inclined to stay folded. But she pressed it down and took the pillow from Jamie's hand and tossed it on the bed and threw down the blanket she had brought in. She nodded to Jamie by way of invitation and told him, "Go to sleep." She had a way of making things sound simpler than they sometimes were, or felt. She lifted Nin off the chair and put her on the bed and said to Jamie, "Go ahead now." Jamie crawled onto the mattress, slightly disappointed, even though he was deeply tired and wanted nothing more than sleep. Nin had never woken up at all.

Jamie could see into the kitchen from where he lay, could see Earl at the stove, making coffee in the spotted blue enamel pot, and his mother, sitting at the table. Jamie smelled the brewing coffee and stared at the legs of the kitchen table and his mother's legs—she called them toothpicks because she thought they were so skinny. He saw a ribbon of her cigarette smoke curl up toward the overhead light with the string pull hanging down from it. He thought he would just close his eyes and listen. He could do that, he didn't have to go to sleep. He liked the sound of their voices, low, liked listening with his eyes closed, and the familiar smells of coffee and cigarette smoke. Once again a Christmasy feeling came over him—of being up late, of getting to fall asleep in a different place, near the grownups, a sense of things, however temporary, being truly different. He remembered the bag of toys, remembered that his mother had brought his magic.

When he woke up, his mother was next to him in the bed and sun was pouring into the room. His mother had slept in her clothes—her jeans and sweatshirt, but not her boots. He leaned up on his elbow to see if she was awake and she instantly shot up, a chain reaction. She gasped and leaned over to check on Nin, whom she had moved to a mound of blankets next to the bed. It was as if she expected Nin to be gone, or dead, the way his mother lunged to check on her, laid her hand across the baby's back, and only then leaned back and relaxed, faced Jamie and whispered, "Hi there."

"Hi," Jamie answered, his voice all dry and filled with sleep. She scooped her arm under his neck and pulled him closer to her.

"Where's Earl?" Jamie asked. It felt late.

"Work, I imagine," she answered. "I can't believe Nin slept straight through."

Jamie could. He could believe it. What

a night she'd had, shooting through the air. Who wouldn't be tired, who wouldn't sleep a long time on a thick pile of blankets, after something like that? His mother kept checking on her, but Jamie knew that Nin was okay.

"Isn't today a school day?" he said. He pulled away from his mother toward his side of the bed.

"For some," she said. She reached over to the arm of the couch for her cigarettes and lighter. "For you and me, though, it's a free day." She flicked the lighter a few times till it caught, lit her cigarette, and took her first drag. "Jamie and Patty Beauville's free day," she said, and exhaled.

Jamie liked the third grade all right, liked his teacher, Mrs. Desrochers, so a free day wasn't as big a deal to him as it would've been the year before, when he had had Mrs. Gimber and everything felt stale and hard and what he knew best was how much he wasn't very good at. It surprised him a little bit, not to be terrifically glad about a free day, and it embarrassed him to admit it, so he didn't.

Jamie went into Earl's scuzzy bathroom to pee and when he came out his mother was still lying in bed smoking and Nin was still asleep. Jamie didn't know what was next. "Where're my clothes?" he asked. Patty pointed over by the door to a pile of stuff Earl had brought in from the car.

He felt nervous getting dressed, in some sort of hurry but for no reason. He fought with his T-shirt, trying to get his arms and head through. His mother was lying on the couch watching him. "Slow down," she told him. "We have the whole day." And after he was dressed she said, "Go on down to the car and get your other bag. The magic."

Yes: that's what Jamie wanted to do, that was the perfect thing to do next. He threw open Earl's front door. The bang of it finally woke Nin up, and he heard her cry as he headed down the stairs. He stepped outside into bright sun, clear, cold air, a gorgeous day, so bright it knocked him back. He wasn't ready for it. It made his eyes ache. His eyes? His head. His heart. Something. Something about the brightness of the day was overwhelming; it gobbled up everything inside itself—everything that had come before and everything that might come next.

Jamie stood still and looked around at the road and the trees and the garage to his side, at the little mountains of gravel and crushed stone, and none of it seemed connected to anything he knew or to anything else, and suddenly he didn't have a clue about where he was. He could have been anywhere, and that felt like nowhere to him. It could have been Texas for all he knew just then. And what was Texas but some extra-big state on a vinyl placemat his father—his real father—had sent him when he was a baby? A map of the United States and a big blue part of it that his mother told him was Texas. Jamie felt surrounded by the immobile tractors and trucks in the yard. No one was around, where was everyone? Dead?

A horrible jumpiness started up in Jamie and he began to hop and shake his hands, thinking it might as well be Texas, or the moon. He caught sight of his mother's Buick, though (Earl had moved it, beyond the piles of sand and gravel), and from what felt like a faraway place Jamie remembered the bag of his stuff—what he'd come for. He raced over to the car and opened the door, reached in and grabbed the pillowcase by its neck, and took off. He didn't even close the car door, just left it open, a flap, a wing, in the sunny, bright day, and tore upstairs again. He burst into the apartment.

His mother was right in front of him, still sitting on the pullout bed, feeding Nin a bottle, and the smoke from her cigarette was all around her, around her face and circling above her head, misty and slightly blue. Like she had just appeared—or was disappearing, which was it?—into or out of smoke, poof, magic, like some trick. "Oh, honey, what is it?" she said, lurching forward as soon as she saw his face.

Just the sound of her voice made a huge difference, all the difference in the world, her voice and now her movement toward him and out of the smoke. Jamie loosened his grip on the neck of the pillowcase.

"Oh, it's okay, sweetie," she said to him,

the same promise she had made to him the night before. "Did something happen? Did you see somebody? Was somebody out there?"

He shook his head, firmed up his lips, and drew his eyebrows together in concentration against crying. He didn't want to cry.

"Catch your breath," his mother told him, and he did.

They heard the downstairs door open and in just a few seconds Earl was walking in on them. "Jamie my man," he said, and held out his palm for Jamie to slap. Earl announced he'd come back to make pancakes. Jamie was glad to hear it, because he liked pancakes and he liked knowing what was next.

EARL MADE UP THE BATTER AND THEN poured big circles of it onto the skillet. "Bigger," Jamie urged, but Earl told him, "He who cooks the pancakes determines their size." The pancakes would be Earl's lunch, their breakfast. Jamie figured that lunchtime was already over at school. They'd be doing math, which he liked, sort of. Spelling was over, he'd slept through that.

Jamie thought what a funny, squirrelly thing time was: how it could be the same time one place as another, even though some people were eating breakfast and some lunch; and how time kept on passing, and things kept on happening, even without him. Things didn't just stop—time didn't—but he still pictured Van standing by the crib, hanging his head.

Patty had moved to the kitchen table and was sitting there, holding Nin, clouded by smoke again. But there was nothing magical or scary about it now—not like when Jamie had burst back into the apartment. It was just his mother, sitting there in cigarette smoke, bouncing Nin and singing, "Trot trot to Boston, trot trot to Lynn."

Jamie got served first and answered "Me" three times when Earl asked, "Who's ready for more?" Part of Jamie wanted never to stop eating, never to have to ask "What's next, what are we doing now?" or to consider that they wouldn't stay right where they were, with Earl, for the rest of their lives.

Jamie had been told so many times and for so long that he must have a tapeworm (something to explain where all that food went) that he'd come to accept it as a fact. He believed that a worm kept him skinny as a rail, believed that it lived inside him and shared all his food. If he could get used to that tapeworm, he figured, then other people probably got used to some pretty awful things too.

When he was finally stuffed, his mother said, "Here, take her," and handed Nin over so that she could eat the rest of her pancakes in peace. Jamie hoped Nin wasn't wet, didn't need to be changed, that he could just put her on the floor in the living room and dangle things around her face to keep her happy. He put her down and played with her for a while, and then went and got a banana and settled into Earl's La-Z-Boy and pulled out his magic book.

It was his all-time favorite book and he read it—studied it—often. The cover had a floppy, draped white glove inside an up-side-down top hat filled with cards and dice. There was a coiled rope and a hand-kerchief and a coin beneath a cup. It was a beautiful cover—the first thing that had attracted Jamie to it at the Littleton book-store. Van had bought it for him, the first time the three of them—Jamie, Van, and Patty—had spent time together and Van was the nicest he would ever be to Jamie. He said he would buy anything Jamie picked out, and Jamie had taken forever choosing. He could tell, when he finally announced his choice, that Van was disap-pointed, because he kept showing him dif-ferent things—books and toys—and saying, "How about this, what about this?" But

Jamie had held firm, and it was the best decision he'd ever made. He had no regrets, the way he sometimes did after he chose a toy or a souvenir or a cookie and then knew almost instantly, as soon as it was out of the package or in his mouth, that he'd made the wrong choice, that the other one—the one he didn't choose—would have been better. The magic book hadn't been like that.

He studied the opening page again, the one that outlined the different kinds of magic: Magic for Fun; Silent Magic; Illusion; Escapology; Mentalism. Escapology had a drawing of someone wriggling free from a tangle of chains, but the caption said you had to learn a lot of techniques and know how to pick locks and that it could be dangerous. Still, it was the one he most wanted to be able to do. He looked at Silent Magic again (that one didn't have a picture—how do you picture silence, any-way?) and read, "Silent acts are performed by the most skilled of all magicians." The majority of acts required patter—the name for what you said during an act or trick—which was discussed on pages 12 and 13. Jamie had been working on his. But silent acts were done without patter.

Jamie remembered the baby flying across the room, shooting across, straight into his mother's arms. He thought about how quiet it was after, dead quiet, until Nin hollered and his mother called out to him. Maybe that was silent magic—the flight and the landing. Maybe he had witnessed the greatest act of all time, and his mother had performed it, with Nin (and with Van, too—Van was definitely in on it).

Earl had to leave and go back to work. He had deliveries to make. "I'll be back," he told them. Jamie's mom said, "And then we'll go see the trailer?" and Earl sighed and said, "Yes, then we'll go see the trailer."

Patty and Jamie and Nin didn't go outside the whole day, for which Jamie was grateful. They just stayed indoors, and when Nin fell asleep on her pile of blankets for her afternoon nap, Jamie and his mother played cards at the kitchen table — double solitaire and gin rummy. Jamie was a terrific card player; his mother said he was one of the greats. When they finished their third game of gin, Patty said to him, "So. What's up, Jamie-boy?" At first he thought she meant did he want to play again, but before he answered he realized she meant something else.

"I don't know," he said. "We're moving." He wasn't sure whether he should deal or wait.

His mother continued. "And why's that?"

Jamie saw Nin flying through the air, a

streak across their bedroom. "I don't know," he said, but he did. He did know. He didn't know how to put it, exactly. He didn't have the words. He didn't want to make his mother remember, or feel bad. The picture in his mind didn't hurt him—he knew it was silent magic—but it might hurt her.

"Take a stab," she said.

Jamie shrugged. He kind of wanted to deal, to start the game. "Van," he said. And then, "Van the man"—the name Jamie had given him before he really knew him, when his mother was just starting to see him, before it wasn't funny. Jamie snuck a little smile at his mother, remembering, and she smiled back. "You know," Jamie said, "because of Nin."

His mother nodded, made a point of her cigarette ash in the ashtray. "Not because," she said. "For. For you and Nin both. I'll find us a place to be and it'll be all right."

After a second she said, "You okay with this?"

Jamie told her he was, and he was, and she said, "Okay, then, deal."

Around three they heard Earl's truck pull in, and he beeped his horn. "Let's go," Patty said, scooping up Nin and grabbing the diaper bag. Jamie got his shoes on, and they tromped down the stairs and outside. The day was as bright as it had been before, but it was all right this time because Jamie was with his mother and Nin, and Earl was waiting for them in his truck, with the door open. All they had to do was climb aboard.

They squished together in the cab of Earl's pickup and his mother pulled the door shut. Earl said, "Patty, this isn't a good idea," to which Patty replied, "Earl, just drive."

THEY ALL RELAXED ON THE DRIVE OUT
to see Earl's trailer. Jamie could tell that
despite what Earl had said about its not
being a good idea, he was glad to be driving
out toward the mountain with everyone
stuffed inside the pickup next to him.
Jamie knew Earl was glad whenever he was
with Patty. It all started to feel like an ad-
venture again—Jamie remembered the
moment of standing on the cement steps in
his pajamas in the middle of the night, remembered the frigid December air across
his feet. Now they had the road to them-

selves and the day was perfect—it was a free day—and his mother had caught the baby. It wasn't Texas, it was Stark, New Hampshire, and Jamie knew it. Even Nin was happy, bouncing along.

Jamie's first sight of the trailer, from a distance, made him think of a big silver toaster. The sunlight hit on it and made it gleam like a jewel—a silver jewel set down at the end of the logging road, slightly tilting toward the trees and the base of the mountain. There was an egg-shaped pond ringed by rocks to the left of the trailer.

"Your own private skating rink," Earl said, and nudged Jamie with his elbow. Jamie, who'd never skated in his life, didn't have an answer, but he liked the idea, and he liked the looks of the place.

Earl had lived there the year before, when he was logging the property for the man in Connecticut who owned it. He'd moved the trailer onto the land when he and June, whom he'd been married to, split up. (Patty told Jamie that Earl and June had "called it quits.") Earl had fixed up the trailer with a generator for electricity and he'd bragged to Patty that he could heat it with a match.

Now, as they approached it, Earl said, "It was fine for *me*," meaning, Jamie could tell, that something about it wouldn't be fine for Patty and Nin and himself—too small, too cold, something—but Jamie could also tell that his mother was sitting there not listening to what Earl was saying, because she was looking at the trailer hard.

Earl pulled his truck up close. He hoisted Nin away from Patty and led them up to the trailer. It was cold as a refrigerator inside, but it was the space more than the climate that struck Jamie—how small it was, how contained. Jamie felt like he was in a box, or a hollowed-out bullet. He was sorry they didn't have their stuff with them then and there—the pillows and blankets and coats his mother had carried out of Van's—because he imagined padding the trailer with everything they owned, imagined the entire little place padded, lined, soft, so that even if a baby went flying, shooting down its tiny interior, there'd be no edges or corners, nothing that could cut or scrape, nothing to smash up against. Anyway, even if someone did go flying, they wouldn't go very far, because there wasn't far to go. Every place was close to every other place. No matter where he stood in the trailer, he was always near somebody else—his mother, or Nin, or Earl.

"Okay," his mother said.

Earl looked at Patty, didn't answer, and walked out the door, down onto the cinderblock step. Patty walked over to stand next to Jamie. "Wha'd'you think?" she asked him.

"I like it," he said. Couldn't she tell?

"So it's all right with you?" she checked again. She didn't usually check twice. Sometimes she made Jamie mad.

"I told you," he said, but that didn't seem to clinch anything either, and Jamie started getting scared that his mother didn't like it, wouldn't let them live there. He started feeling scrootchy all over, like his body was going to start hopping away from him. He pictured Van standing by the crib, and it was hard holding him still, hard to keep his hand on the crib. "What'll we do if we don't move here?" Jamie asked. "Live nowhere?"

Patty turned and looked at Jamie, zoomed in on him so that Jamie's whole world was her face, her eyes looking at him. "Is that what you're thinking, Jamie?

You're thinking that just because we left Van we won't have any place to live? You think we'll be homeless? What, you think we'll end up living in the car or something?" She took in her breath like she wished she could draw back every bad thing that had happened so far. She closed her eyes and pursed her lips and breathed. Jamie was going to get a stomach ache.

"Jamie," she said, when she opened her eyes, "I'll find us a place to live, I am *finding* us a place to live, that's what I'm doing, finding us a place. See? We're here, right now. We'll have a place, you don't have to worry about that. Okay? And Earl will help us. You don't have to worry, okay?"

Jamie nodded, and whatever had been tightest and scariest between them broke up. "Mr. Worrier," Patty said, and she put her hand on the top of his head. "Mr. Worry Wart." She pulled him in closer and rubbed his back. "You hear me?" she said. "Okay?"

Jamie said, "Yeah," and Patty said, "All right then, all right." The trailer was so cold they could see their breath. After a while they went and stood with Earl and Nin in front of the trailer, at the base of Percy Peak.

"So you gonna let me have it?" Jamie's mother said to Earl.

Earl shook his head. "Pats," he said. "It's not a question of letting you have it. You know I'd give it to you in a second. But lookit," he said, gesturing out to all the space around them, filled with nothing but sky, trees, the mountain, the old logging road. Jamie thought how beautiful it was. "There's nothing here," Earl said. "You'll be sitting ducks."

Jamie didn't know what ducks had to do with anything.

"Is that a no?" Patty was lighting up a cigarette.

"No, it's not a no," he said. (Jamie knew that a no was never really a no with Earl.) "Why don't you just stay at my place in town?" Earl tried.

Jamie's mom didn't say anything to Earl, but she gave him a look.

"I could move out," he offered. "Stay with June for a while. She wouldn't mind."

"Like hell she wouldn't," Patty said.

They all stood there for a minute. Patty reached over and took Nin back from Earl. "You'll be sitting ducks," Earl said one more time, more sad than anything else.

"Yes or no?" Patty said.

Earl shook his head again and gave up. "All right," he said, "if that's really what you want to do."

Jamie's heart soared. The trailer was theirs, all theirs in the middle of nowhere.

They could move their stuff in, they could heat it with a match, they could sit like ducks. He started jumping up and down, held out his palm for Earl to slap him five.

They piled back into the truck and headed down the bumpy logging road. Jamie turned around to look at the silver trailer, getting smaller as they pulled away, tilting in the sun, leaning toward the base of the mountain, leaning the way he and his mother were—away from how things had been for a long time.

THEY MOVED IN THE NEXT DAY. IT
didn't take long, because they didn't have
much. Jamie's mom said that with what
Earl had left behind and what she had carried away, they'd make do. She said the only
thing they really needed was Nin's crib.

But no one made a move to go get it,
and Patty made a bed for Nin in the pulled-
out drawer of an old bureau of Earl's. She
lined the drawer with a big pillow wrapped
in a baby blanket, and it was perfect. Jamie
thought it was wonderful, better than any
crib. When he thought of Nin's crib, he

pictured Van standing beside it, and he wanted his mother never to go back. He would have liked a drawer big enough for himself, but he slept in the only real bed they had, a less-than-double mattress in the little room in the back of the trailer, and Patty slept in the recliner chair, tilted back as far as it would go.

Sitting at the kitchen table where Jamie and his mother played cards, he had a perfect view of Nin sleeping in her drawer. Lots of times he imagined snapping the drawer shut and making her disappear if he ever needed to. He remembered a movie on TV once that showed an apartment where the bed folded down, out from the wall. He thought that was neat, too, thought it would make another great hiding place—though when he thought about a person actually using it, he imagined him squished against the wall, a pancake person, like in the cartoons. He was pretty sure that Nin would fit, no problem, with the drawer pushed in, if he had to close it in a hurry. He was pretty sure she'd be able to breathe. Or he could punch little holes in the bottom of the drawer above it, the way he did on the lids for jars he used to trap caterpillars and spiders and bugs. He didn't do those things, snap the drawer shut or drill any holes—he just thought about how he could if he had to, because of Van.

Mostly Jamie didn't think about Van. Van wasn't there. *They* were there—Nin and his mother and himself—and the trailer fit them just right. Jamie had other things to think about. He wanted his mother to take him to the Groveton Christmas Carnival and Fair.

"Why can't we go?" he started.

She told him to quit bugging her.

"But why can't we?"

"Because we're poor," she said. She asked him if he'd seen any envelopes stuffed with dollar bills lying around the trailer, begging to be spent on games and presents and fried dough. When Jamie answered, "No," she said, "All right, then."

But she took him anyway—on Friday night, to celebrate the end of what Patty called "the week that was." She wanted to take Nin, too, but Jamie talked her out of it. He pointed out that Nin was too little to eat the food, to play the games, to win anything. Jamie could practically feel his mother walking slower because of her, stopping to make sure she wasn't too hot or too cold in all her blankets, saying it was time to go if Nin's fussing got bad. Finally Patty said, "Oh, all right, I suppose Agnes won't mind." Agnes was Van's mother, but she and Van didn't have anything to do with each other, and she babysat Nin for

Patty when Patty needed her to. Sometimes Agnes babysat for Jamie too, after school, when Patty had to work—she had a part-time job bagging groceries at the IGA. Jamie liked Agnes all right, and she was nice to him, but it embarrassed him to feel sorry for a grownup, the way he did for Agnes, about having a son like Van.

When they stopped in Groveton to drop Nin off at Agnes' house, Jamie wouldn't even get out of the car, didn't want to slow things down one more minute than they had to. "Just drop her," he urged his mother. "Off."

Patty was still rooting around in the back seat, lifting Nin out of her carseat and hoisting the bag stuffed with diapers and wipes and bottles. She looked up at Jamie and said, "You could just hold your horses a little bit, you know."

But she didn't take as long as she some-

times did—because Agnes was a talker—
and they got to the high school in Groveton
around seven-thirty. The parking lot was already full. Patty pulled the car over the edge
of the blacktop onto the adjoining field and
frozen grass crunched beneath the car
wheels. Jamie flew out of the car. It was
cold and dark and there still had been no
snow at all—the first winter of Jamie's life
that there hadn't been snow by December.

He ran on ahead to the main entrance,
went in, and followed construction paper
arrows to the Christmas carnival. The gym-
nasium was a container of sound, noise
ricocheting off the walls and bleachers.
Jamie stood on the threshold for just a second, on the lip of the polished blond floor
with its painted lines, and studied all the
little booths that had been set up. There
were a lot of people, a lot of kids running
around, lots of little crocheted things. All

Jamie cared about, really, was the games. He wanted to toss, shoot, aim, choose lucky numbers, win. He hadn't known before just then that that's what he'd come for, but standing at the entrance, everything spread out before him like it was on a platter, he knew it was the games he wanted most.

He went to the booth closest to him: a ring toss game. The back panel was draped with a black and orange and green afghan that would be raffled off on Sunday. A few stuffed animals were pinned to the blanket, and an oak-tag sign said three rings for five tickets.

Jamie's mother came up behind him — she'd bought a long tongue of paper tickets and was folding them up — and asked him if he was sure he wanted this game, if he didn't want to check out the others first before he decided, because they couldn't play every one. He knew that, he knew that. But he had to have this one right now, before he did anything else. He couldn't see or hear or talk or think until he'd done this one. His mother tore off five of the tickets and handed them to the woman running the booth—a large woman who wore a long sweater with deep pockets. She was so heavy that just taking the tickets and handing over the rings made her pant a little.

Jamie was all ready to send the little rubber circles flying, right onto the cones. And they did fly right out of his hands, all three of them, before he knew it, before he even felt them or planned or thought, they just went spinning right out of his hands, toward the cones, one, two—the first two sailing straight past the cone they were supposed to land on—and three. The third one got snagged by the tip of the cone and settled across its top.

"I did it, I did it!" He was yelling. The

black ring crowning the cone was so beautiful a sight to him, so absolutely perfect, that he choked a little bit. The woman who was running the game reached under her chair and pulled out a cardboard box filled with small, plastic-wrapped stuffed animals. She handed one to Jamie. It was no giant panda bear, not even the size of the animals pinned to the corners of the afghan, but Jamie didn't mind. He handed it straight to his mother. She could keep it, she could give it to Nin. His success made him wildly generous. All he really wanted was another game, another shot at something.

"How about something to eat?" his mother asked, and he could hear her, finally. "Okay," he said, and they walked to the back of the gym and got hot dogs and cans of soda. He ate his too fast, drank down the soda in slugs that made him burp, but he wanted to play more games—they were calling to him like a race that had already started and that he was supposed to run in, fast as he could, that he could maybe even win.

A bunch of kids from his class at school were there. He saw his teacher, Mrs. Desrochers, but he pretended not to see her until she called out to him and waved. He played almost every game there was to play, then had another hot dog and a snow cone.

The noise was a big, deafening envelope around them. Jamie had no idea of time at all, what it was, how much of it had passed. Every now and then his mother would come and find him and tell him they had to go soon. Finally she caught his eye and held up her finger. "One more," she mouthed to him. He pointed to the back of the gym and they both walked down.

In the farthest corner, fenced off by

sawhorses, a booth was set up with a BB gun and a moving target—little yellow tin ducks grinding along a black rotating belt. The sign taped to the back wall spelled out in fat, black letters: **SITTING DUCKS.** As Jamie approached the booth he watched their slow progress along the stretch of black, watched them reach the curve and travel upside down along the bottom until they made their grinding ascent at the other side and rose to pass before him again. The game was to shoot them. The BB gun was mounted on a wooden stand about six feet back from the ducks, and eight tickets got you three shots as they plodded along the conveyor belt. If you hit one, it bent back sideways, laid parallel to the belt instead of upright. It was such a good game that there weren't even any prizes. Just doing it was enough.

"This one," Jamie said. He turned to beg

his mother, even if it had to be the last. "This one." There was a line, and he could scarcely stand having to wait. He did, though—waited and watched while the three guys in front of him took their turn and pinged the ducks, snapped them flat back against the conveyor belt. It didn't look hard at all; it looked like the easiest thing in the world.

Finally it was Jamie's turn. He was barely tall enough to hold the gun level to the box it was mounted on and see through the sight to aim. He pulled himself up as far as he could go.

The man running the game asked him, "You gonna be able to handle that, son?" Jamie just nodded, scared to add words about whether he was too young or too small. Instead, he put all his concentration into hoisting and balancing the gun, holding it steady, waiting for the next slow-moving, grinding duck to proceed straight into his sight. He fired, ping, and down it went. He was so excited by what he'd done that he took his next shot right away, and missed. He made himself wait before he took the third one, his last. He let two more ducks grind by, slow as molasses, right there in perfect, easy sight, and held back until he was absolutely sure he had it. Then he fired, and with that neat pinging sound that had been part of the noise all night, the duck snapped back.

Jamie spun around to see that his mother had seen, and she had, but she was already nodding, saying, "Okay, that's it, that's all now, you did it, you did a real good job." He could barely hear. Maybe he asked her for one more time, one more round, but she wasn't budging, and he was done anyway, he'd gotten plenty.

She said, "Come on, now," and they

started walking down the length of the gym, toward the exit. Jamie was bouncing along, flying high from his success, when suddenly Patty grabbed his hand, spun him around, and yanked him over to the snow cone stand. She pulled him so hard and so suddenly that he almost fell.

"Mom," he cried out, but she said "No" in such a furious, frantic whisper that it practically sent his word right back down his throat, and then, with another yank, she had them crouching by the side of the stand. Patty's eyes were huge and Jamie turned to see what she might be looking at. At first he couldn't find anything at all, but then he did see: Van—his back, walking along the bleachers. Both Patty and Jamie watched him, frozen to their spot, hiding. They watched him like a scary movie as he walked to the farthest corner of the gym, to where they'd just been, and then watched as he turned and looked back in their direction.

It wasn't Van. It wasn't Van at all, the dark-haired man with the pug face who turned around and looked back. Not even close. Jamie's mouth dropped open with surprise, and he turned to his mother, but her surprise had already changed into something else.

She stood quickly and pulled Jamie up with her. She brushed herself off, as if she'd fallen or tripped. Jamie thought she tried to stand up taller than she actually was. She flicked her hair like they hadn't just been hiding. Jamie looked at her, then looked around them. The snow cone lady was busy scratching up ice into a paper cup, but some of the people in line were looking at Jamie and his mother. Mrs. Desrochers, Jamie's teacher, was in that line, and she was looking at them.

"Okay," his mother said, and walked tall to the door, but when they got outside, she forgot where she'd parked the car, and they had to wander for a while, looking.

6

On the way home, the car felt dark and cavernous to Jamie, and completely filled with his mother's silence. "Did you bring the dog I won?" he finally asked, just to break it.

"I brought it," she answered him right back, as if she were mad at him for asking. Her tone made him scared to continue. But the silence was scarier than anything. "I'm gonna give it to Nin," he said. "She can have it in her drawer. We can tell her I won it when she's bigger."

Nothing.

"Good thing we didn't bring Nin

tonight," he tried. Jamie thought that then was the perfect time for his mother to say, "Thanks to you," but she didn't—she didn't say a word. And her not answering left him all alone to think how he—Jamie—how he'd been the one who'd saved Nin from going to the fair in the first place and running into someone who even looked like Van. And he ached to say that, to point out how he'd been the one to keep Nin away, safe and sound with Agnes, but there was no room for him to say it, no door to walk through, and so the words and the need to say them just sat inside him along with the hot dogs and soda and snow cone he'd eaten. Patty was driving fast, and Jamie didn't try to talk again.

At Agnes' house, Patty said, "Wait here," and left Jamie alone. How different the car felt without Patty in it. Worse? Better? Different.

Patty got Nin in record time. She settled her in her carseat and then hopped back in next to Jamie and thunked the car into reverse. Jamie kept remembering the night they left Van's. But why? It hadn't even been Van this time. No one went flying. It wasn't the same at all. Things were better but they felt worse. His mother wasn't the same either. She wasn't saying, "It's all right, we're all right." His mother was worse.

She didn't slow down, even when they hit the logging road and the car went rolling in and out of the ruts. Jamie felt like the inside of his body was going to separate from the outside.

As soon as they got in the trailer Patty turned on the lights and snapped on the radio, and got Nin bedded down in her little drawer and gave her a bottle and walked over to the cupboard and got herself out a new pack of cigarettes. She was doing everything fast, even when she stood still, rubbing her middle finger against her thumb (the hand that wasn't holding the cigarette).

Jamie stood and watched her. Finally she looked up and saw him and said, "What? Who're you looking at?" So mean. As mean as she could be. Jamie wheeled around, away, like he'd been caught at something bad, like he'd been slapped, and as he turned he caught just a flash of blue out of the corner of his eye—the blue of the ear of the dog he'd won at the fair, still in its plastic, that Patty had put next to Nin in her drawer. And without thinking, without any plan at all, Jamie lunged over to the drawer and kicked it.

Would it slide right in, just the way he'd imagined? Would she disappear, would she be able to breathe? He did it so fast—the spin, the kick—and of course nothing happened the way he'd ever thought it might. All his kick did was startle Nin awake, rock the drawer, make the little dog in plastic jump, and then Nin was squalling and his mother was yelling, everything at the same time.

"What are you doing? What are you *doing*?" She had her hands on Jamie's shoulders. "What?" she screamed in his face. "Van wasn't enough, now *you* have to start this shit?" She shook him once, hard, dropped her hands off his shoulders, and spun around to pick up Nin.

Jamie turned and stepped into the bathroom. He vomited before he even reached the toilet—threw up on the floor, and then stepped in his own vomit as he reached the sink, still throwing up, everything he'd eaten, everything he'd been given, pushing out of him just the way he'd pushed it all in. He threw up until his ribs hurt and his legs were shaking, and sometime while it was happening he felt his mother's hands around his waist, across his back, and heard her saying, "Oh my baby, my poor baby."

Even when there was nothing left to throw up, Jamie still hung his head over the sink, stunned by everything that had happened, the whole night, what it all was. His mother got a washcloth. She wet it under the shower, wrung it out, folded it, and put it against Jamie's forehead and then across each cheek. The cool moisture was an amazing sensation, like a whole new season: spring after so much winter, or real autumn after summer heat. She was still talking to him—"You poor kid, I'm sorry, Jesus, I'm sorry." But it was the sound of her voice that he heard more than the words—it was her real voice. So he had her voice and the feel of the washcloth, its coolness and the nubbly texture of the cloth itself.

She moved him out of the bathroom and away from the vomit. "Let's get you undressed," she said, and he obeyed, raising his arms up so she could pull his shirt over his head, just the way she always did when he was little, pulling off his shoes, his socks, and then his pants, his underpants. He stood naked while she went to his bed and grabbed his pajamas from under his pillow and brought them to him. She helped him step inside the pants; Jamie rested his hand on her shoulder to balance himself. She even buttoned the shirt buttons, and the material of his pajamas was incredibly soft against his skin. And then she led him over to his bed and he climbed in and sank into it. Usually he felt bad about taking the bed and knowing his mother would take the chair, fall asleep in the recliner and wake up stiff, but tonight he didn't, he didn't think about that or anything at all. His mother leaned over to kiss him good night and he surprised them both when he looked up and asked, "What happened?"

His mother stared at him and then repeated what he'd said. "What happened." She sat down on the side of his bed, and when she sighed, her body released and slumped in on itself. For a while she didn't say anything at all and Jamie might have gone to sleep for just a second, but then she said, "What happened is we got scared. We got scared." She turned and looked at him hard.

"Oh God, Jamie," she said, "we're afraid—just sick with fear. And it's so settled inside us that we don't even know what living feels like without it. That must be the thing about fear, the trick of it—you forget that that's what it is because it just starts to feel like your life. We're afraid, Jamie.

That's all we are. And if we don't get past it, we'll be hiding from strangers and throwing up in the sink until the day we die."

CHAPTER

. . . .

7

For the rest of the weekend after the fair, after they saw the man who wasn't even Van, Jamie and Patty and Nin didn't go anywhere at all. They planted themselves inside the trailer. Patty and Jamie played cards and lay around and drank soda. It was like they were all getting over the flu or something.

Jamie began pretending that he and his mother and Nin were the only people left on earth. Everyone else was dead, blasted by a bomb, and only they had escaped. (Except Earl. Earl had survived, too, and he would come and visit them sometimes and bring them food and other things that they needed. His job was to go and find things that weren't contaminated.) It was such an easy world for Jamie to go off into, from safe inside their trailer that had dropped out of the sky, and the bruise-purple mountain behind them.

When Monday came and it was time for school, he wasn't ready to go. He was too far away. "I'm not going," he told his mother.

"Why not?" she asked him, but he could tell that she didn't have the heart for it either. Maybe she knew that everything was bombed out, that they were all that was left anyway. "Are you sick?" she asked. "You still sick?"

Jamie nodded. Yeah, that was it. He was still sick.

They drove to the package store to use

the phone—Patty called in sick to the IGA—and they stayed home together Monday and Tuesday. By Wednesday Patty didn't even bother to ask Jamie how he felt in the morning, and he didn't bother to say, and they went through the rest of the week that way.

Jamie practiced his magic tricks a lot. When Nin was awake, he put her in her little yellow seat that rocked, and performed for her. He started every performance with the rabbit ears—the first trick he'd ever learned, from a waiter in a restaurant in Plymouth, New Hampshire.

The waiter had shown Jamie how to hold and fold the napkin so that at the end he could pull out two floppy ears. Jamie thought he had the trick down cold, because he did it, no problem, at the restaurant, over and over again, even while Patty was telling him that was enough, to get going on his hamburger. But on the way home, in the car, he got confused about what to do first, which end to pull, and the more he tried the more he forgot until finally he had nothing at all to hold on to, to work with.

"Give it a rest," his mother had told him.

But he couldn't, and all of a sudden a feeling had come into his body, like his bones were bigger than his skin, and when he started kicking it was a surprise to him, because his legs were doing it on their own, without him. He kicked the window handle so hard that he broke it, and Patty swerved the car over to the breakdown lane and came to a stop. Jamie waited for her to yell at him, to say that they would sit there until he could calm down, or maybe that she would just leave him on the side of the road and he could walk all the way back to

Stark, but she didn't. She looked at him a long time and finally said, "You really do have to know, don't you?" And she turned the car around and drove half an hour to Plymouth so they could find the waiter and have him show Jamie all over again.

Now he began every magic show with that trick he would never forget. He was doing it Monday morning when Patty said something about getting ready for school. Jamie said he was still sick. "You are not," she told him, but she didn't push past it, and Jamie didn't miss a beat in pulling out the rabbit ears.

He thought they could just go on that way, staying home together and playing cards and practicing his magic, but the very next afternoon, when Nin was sleeping and Jamie and Patty were playing double solitaire, Jamie's teacher, Mrs. Desrochers, paid them a visit.

They saw a car—a huge green Bonneville—pull onto their road, and watched in silence as it approached. When it got close enough, Jamie recognized Mrs. Desrochers and willed her, with whatever power he possessed, to turn around, go back, and leave them alone.

"Who is that?" Patty finally said, when Mrs. Desrochers stepped out of the car and started walking toward the trailer. She was a big woman, made even bigger by her puffy parka, and she looked soft and tough at the same time.

"My teacher," Jamie said, and he turned to face his mother. He could feel both their hearts sink.

There was a knock on the door. "It's Alma Desrochers," she called out. "Can I come in?"

Patty stood up and said, "Just a minute," shrugged, and then said, "Yeah, come on in."

"Thank you" was the first thing Mrs. Desrochers said to Patty's face. Then her name again: "I'm Alma Desrochers, Jamie's teacher. Hello, Jamie," and she nodded in his direction.

Patty answered, "Jamie told me." Jamie could feel his mother on his side, against Mrs. Desrochers being there.

"I've missed you, Jamie," she said. "Have you been sick?"

Jamie looked to his mother to see what sort of answer might do the trick.

"We've both been under the weather," Patty said.

Mrs. Desrochers said she was sorry to hear that, and that she hoped they were feeling better. "I'm sorry to just sort of show up," she continued, "but I know you don't have a phone, and there was something I wanted to talk to you about if you have a minute."

Patty said okay, but Jamie knew she was hating it as much as he was—and he even liked Mrs. Desrochers. He was remembering that just then, that he actually liked her, the way she didn't make him feel stupid. She just wasn't supposed to be there.

"You visit all the kids in your class who get sick?" Patty said. She sounded to Jamie like she was trying to pick a fight.

"No," Mrs. Desrochers told her. "I don't. Just the missing in action."

"Listen," Patty told her, "this is a good place for us, we don't need any help. Jamie's safe here."

"I believe you," Mrs. Desrochers said, and after she said it, it was like there was nothing Patty could say back. The fight Patty was trying to pick was a fire that couldn't get started, and Jamie didn't know what would happen next. "He's safe with me too," his teacher said.

Patty didn't answer, then looked at Jamie and said, "Why don't you watch some TV." Earl had rigged one up for them—it had terrible reception, but it was something.

Jamie shrugged. He wanted to listen, but he didn't want to be there. Or he didn't want her to be there. Things were mixed up.

Mrs. Desrochers and Patty sat down at the kitchen table. There were still the long, crooked rows of cards, red on black on red, from Jamie and Patty's unfinished game of double solitaire.

Jamie clicked on the set and the screen filled with static.

He heard Mrs. Desrochers say, "Jamie needs to be in school if I'm going to find a way in." She made a gesture like she was jiggling a doorknob. "I believe there's a way in or I wouldn't teach. But I need my kids to show up."

Patty tensed when Mrs. Desrochers said

the last part, about showing up. "Like I said," she told her, "we've been under the weather." She reached for her cigarettes.

"I take it that it's been bad weather," Mrs. Desrochers said.

Jamie had the TV on but he was still listening hard. He knew how Mrs. Desrochers talked to people, how she didn't say things as if there was an answer and she was the only one who had it. She was going to talk that way to Patty—she already was—and Patty would go over to her. Jamie knew that.

Patty's laugh was a little snort. "You could say that," Patty agreed. "Real lousy weather." Jamie looked at his mother and Mrs. Desrochers sitting in the late afternoon sunlight that was pouring through the window, drenching them.

He turned up the TV a little louder. There was nothing good on. Why was Mrs.

Desrochers there? What was she doing at the trailer? She belonged at school. He didn't like having the two places mixed up together, the way he didn't like potatoes and meat on the same forkful. He liked things separate. He flicked the channel dial faster and faster, and every one was only static and snow.

"Take it easy, Jamie," Patty said to him. "Why don't you go outside and run around?" He didn't answer her, just kept turning the dial.

"He gets jumpy," Patty explained to Mrs. Desrochers.

"Don't we all," Mrs. Desrochers said. A moment later she asked, "Are you here by yourselves?"

Patty said, "That's right, all by our lonesome."

"Jamie's father?" Mrs. Desrochers asked.

"Oh, he's long gone," Patty said. "It's

Nin's father who's not here." She nodded over to the drawer where Nin was still sleeping. "Not here but might as well be. Kind of like living with a ghost."

Jamie turned up the TV as loud as it would go, as if that would make the picture clear.

"Okay, that's it," Patty said. "Turn it down. Turn it off. Outside, Jamie. Go outside." His mother pointed to the door.

He looked at them both—his mother and his teacher—sitting there in his trailer, by his card game, and then snapped off the television and bolted outside.

He stood still for a few seconds in what Earl had called the middle of nowhere. The mountains were a sad and beautiful dusty rose color, and the sun was going down. There still wasn't any snow. Then, for no reason, he began to run—a loop around the trailer, and then another, and another. He picked up speed as he ran and it didn't take long before he was winded, and stopped, and wanted to go inside again.

And even though he'd been gone only a few minutes, as soon as he stepped back into the trailer, still panting, he could tell that he'd missed out on something. His mother seemed lighter, somehow—but he didn't know what it was that had been lifted from her, or how Mrs. Desrochers had done it, and he didn't like not knowing.

Mrs. Desrochers was getting ready to leave and she said to Patty, "I'm serious about having Jamie stay with me on Tuesday afternoons," and his mother nodded and said, "Yeah, well, thanks." They could have been speaking Spanish for all Jamie knew; they could have been standing in Texas while he was miles away in New Hampshire.

"I've missed you," Mrs. Desrochers told him again. "It'll be nice to have you back."

And as soon as Mrs. Desrochers had

pulled out of sight in her big green Bonneville his mother told him, "You have to
go back to school, Jamie."

How he hated her then. Why would his
mother send him away from the trailer,
back to the exploded, contaminated world?
Why couldn't they just stay together the
way they had been and Earl could bring
them food sometimes?

"I mean it, Jamie," his mother said, but
she didn't need to say it because he knew
she meant it, he could tell. Whatever had
happened to make his mother feel better
was already making him feel worse. "She's
all right," Patty said. "She'll help us."

"Help us what?" Jamie wanted to know.
Did they need help?

"Oh, Jamie," his mother said. "You know.
Just help, give us a hand." She was about to
say something else when she spotted the
bookbag Mrs. Desrochers had left behind

on the kitchen chair. "Oh, she'll be need-
ing that," she said. Her energy made
Jamie's head hurt. "I can probably catch
her," Patty said, grabbing it. "I'll try and
catch her," she said again. "You stay here
with Nin and I'll be right back, okay?"

Jamie didn't answer. Why should he?

"Okay, Jamie?" Patty said again, but she
was already out the door, already leaving,
like it was the most important thing in the
world to get Mrs. Desrochers' stupid bag to
her. Jamie wouldn't answer his mother.

"I'll be right back," she said again.

He wouldn't even look at her driving out
the road. He didn't look up until the car
was gone — had turned off the logging road,
out of sight. And when he looked up and
it was gone, it was as if his mother's car
had never been there, and as if she were
gone forever. He could hardly believe how
empty the road was, and the side of the

road, all the way up to the trailer. He walked over to Nin's drawer and looked hard at her sleeping. She was there, all right, but when he looked up his mother was not. She was gone. The jumpiness came over him again, the same as when Mrs. Desrochers had arrived and started talking to his mother, but it was worse this time, and spreading all through him. He remembered his mother's voice telling him, "Go outside, Jamie," and that voice was all there was—everything else was gone—and he bolted out of the trailer and began running. He ran as fast as his heart was beating, so fast that he couldn't take in how empty everything was, how gone the car was, how it was never coming back. He ran and ran and ran, even when the stitch in his side became a knife.

Jamie was past seeing or hearing any-thing when his mother pulled onto the logging road. He never saw her stop the car, jump out and run toward him, drop to her knees and open her arms. He never saw her at all until he collided with her, nearly pushed her straight back. She clutched him hard against her. "Oh my God, my baby, oh baby, what is it?" And then she lifted him up like he *was* a baby and carried him inside the trailer and laid him down on the bed.

It wasn't until then, until Jamie was on his back on his bed and his mother was leaning over him and stroking his face, brushing the hair away from his eyes, that Jamie understood that his mother was there, that she wasn't gone forever and ever after all. And no sooner did he know that, did it register inside his body, than he pulled back and kicked her, kicked Patty with all his might.

8

CHRISTMAS WAS COMING NO MATTER what.

Jamie couldn't help how much he wanted it. He marked every trick in the magic catalogue that he wished he had. Patty told him he'd save a whole lot of ink if he just circled the few things he didn't want.

And even though she kept telling Jamie they didn't have much money to spend, Patty planned a shopping trip to Littleton for Saturday morning. Friday night the thermometer dropped to -29 degrees, and by nine the next morning it was still only 15 below.

Patty got everyone loaded into the frozen car, and then Jamie and Nin sat in the back seat while Patty tried again and again to get it to start, and the more she tried the more tired and slow the engine sounded. Jamie knew it was dying—all you had to do was listen to know that it was getting worse—but he didn't say anything, and they just sat there while Patty held the key and pumped the pedal, and they listened to it die. Then Patty put her head on the steering wheel and sighed and said, "When is this going to stop?" Her voice sounded like it was coming from some deep well.

Jamie sat as still as could be and didn't know what to do. His mother was crying.

"Want me to look under the hood?" he said. He didn't know what he would do once he looked under the hood, but that's what Van did, and Earl did. They lifted up the hood.

Patty turned and looked at him and smiled even though she was still crying. "Oh, honey, we wouldn't even know what we were looking for," she said. "Come on," and she got Nin out of her car seat and they trooped back to the trailer. She had stopped crying and later all she said was, "It's just as well we couldn't go. No damn money anyway."

Still, Christmas was coming. No matter what, it was coming and Jamie wanted it. He wanted a tree, too. Last year had been bad with the tree—Van had made a big deal out of finding and cutting down the biggest one he could, and when he couldn't get it through the door he'd gotten ugly. But that was last December, and now, one year later, a week before Christmas, Jamie wanted to know, "When are we gonna get one?" It seemed to him that time was running out.

His mother was sitting at the table, smoking. "We're surrounded by trees, Jamie-boy," she said, gesturing to the outside around them. "Take your pick." So Jamie picked one out—a small and perfect tree just a stone's throw from the trailer—and Patty commended him on his choice and then told him that they'd decorate it right there, where it stood, because she wasn't about to chop down a tree and haul it inside just so it could die. He was torn—part of him said the tree had to be inside with them, but part of him really did like it right there, where it belonged.

Jamie and Patty strung popcorn that night, and Jamie made ornaments out of the pictures he had circled from the magic catalogue. He glued them on pieces of cardboard and made hooks out of untwisted paper clips. He begged his mother to buy tinsel, but she told him to forget it and bunch up pieces of tin foil instead. Bit by bit the next day they dressed up the outside tree Jamie had chosen. Sometimes it looked dumb to him and sometimes it looked beautiful. He could see the tree when he was sitting inside the trailer by the little kitchen window, and when the tin foil caught the sun it shot out a thrilling explosion of sparkles that startled Jamie again and again.

Monday morning, when he was walking down the logging road to meet the school bus, the wind lifted one of his magic trick ornaments off its branch, held it spinning in the air, and then wooshed it away, out of sight, as Jamie watched. He didn't mind, seeing it fly off. During the whole long, bumpy ride to school he pictured his magic trick zooming along, on its way to somewhere else.

He only had two more days and then he'd be out for vacation. Patty had been true to her word and sent Jamie off on the bus every single morning, even though it felt like dying to him some days, leaving Patty and Nin in the trailer, going off to that other place.

It wasn't that Mrs. Desrochers said anything, or made a big deal over him, or even gave him a break, but he could feel her just waiting for a chance to step in closer. Jamie didn't know what would happen if Mrs. Desrochers stepped in closer. But he remembered the way she'd broken through to Patty, as if she had melted her insides or something.

Mrs. Desrochers and his mother had even cooked up a plan where Jamie would stay late at school on Tuesday afternoons so that Patty could go to some meeting in Groveton. Patty said the meeting was a group of women who were trying real hard and needed to talk about it. "I know you're not crazy about the arrangement," Patty told him when she handed him his lunchbox on Tuesday morning, "but it's the best I can do."

So on the last day of school before vacation began, four days before Christmas, Jamie stayed late with Mrs. Desrochers while his mother went to Groveton. He sat at his desk, and every time she asked if he wanted to do something—help her water the plants, try out a book from the library— he said no. His mother had packed extra peanut butter crackers in his lunch and he was going to sit and eat those. Mrs. Desrochers stayed at the back of the room, tending all the plants she kept there—her Christmas cactus and night-blooming cereus, the peace lily and all her baby spider plants. Out of nowhere she asked Jamie if he'd given any thought to presents. He thought it was a pretty stupid question, because of course he had given plenty of thought to all the things he wanted: all those magic tricks, hanging and dancing on the branches of the tree, beneath the clumps of tin foil. It turned out that she meant presents *from* him, though—for Nin and his mother.

He didn't turn around to answer Mrs. Desrochers, just kept chewing. "No damn money," he finally answered, and then waited to hear if he could get away with what he'd said: his mother's very own words.

"And where does that leave you?" Mrs. Desrochers said.

Jamie shrugged. "Nin's too little for good toys anyway." He didn't say that he considered his magic tricks a kind of present, his very own gift to Nin—hours and hours of his concentrated attention, the handkerchief trick, the nickels-into-dimes trick, over and over. He actually couldn't believe how good Nin had it. It wasn't that he thought he was so great, just that Nin was lucky to be exposed to so much magic, almost on a daily basis.

"How about your mother?" she asked. "Have you thought about what she might like?"

A car. The first thing Jamie thought was: a car. He thought of their big stupid car and listening to the engine grind and grind on its way to dying, and the way she put her head on the steering wheel. A brand-new, start-every-time car for his mother, red or bright blue, like an ornament. He stuffed another cracker in his mouth.

Or a bed. She needed a bed, her own real bed, with fat pillows and a bedspread, and a little table next to it with a drawer for her cigarettes. But how would they get a bed through the door, the narrow door of their trailer? It would never fit, the same as the Christmas tree that didn't fit, that one that Van sent flying.

Money. His mouth was so full of crackers and peanut butter that he was barely able to chew. He imagined dollars—hundreds of them—attached with paper clips to their outside Christmas tree, dancing and twirling alongside the pictures of the magic tricks, so many of them that even when the wind grabbed some up and carried them away, there were always plenty left behind, enough for all the cars and beds and tricks in the world. He forced the last peanut butter cracker into his mouth.

Suddenly, out of nowhere, there was a hand on his shoulder. He shot up in his seat and whirled around, his body tense as wire. The crackers turned to sand in his mouth.

But it was only Mrs. Desrochers, standing there with a little potted Christmas cactus in her hand, already saying she was sorry, that she hadn't meant to scare him.

She had, though — scared him. Or something had. And once it started up in Jamie it was hard to come back from it.

He turned away from her and managed to swallow and not choke. Mrs. Desrochers took a step back and waited. "I'm sorry I scared you," she said again. "My husband surprised me once when I was vacuuming and I just about had a heart attack."

Finally Jamie shrugged and said that it was no big deal.

"I wondered if you'd thought about giving your mother a plant." She held out the small cactus between them, its pointy leaves loaded with teardrop-shaped buds, some of them already opening into rich, pink-red blooms.

Jamie studied the plant in its dark green plastic container.

"Yours for the asking," Mrs. Desrochers offered.

"It's kinda small," he finally answered, but even as he said so, he knew his mother would love it, and so he went ahead and asked.

Like many true surprises, the first winter storm to hit Stark came in the night. It struck two days before Christmas and covered every exposed thing with a delicate but strong layer of ice.

Patty and Jamie and Nin awoke to it, the iced-over world outside, and for Jamie it was nothing but magic. But when Patty discovered that the storm had sealed the trailer door shut so that she couldn't even push it open, she leaned her head against the door and pounded her fists on it.

She tried kicking the door open, even

got a knife from the utensil drawer and tried breaking the coating of ice that had sealed the cracks. She stopped only when Nin woke up and started hollering. "Might as well live at the damn North Pole," she said, slamming the knife back in the drawer.

Jamie didn't see what was so bad about the North Pole, or even about being stuck in the trailer. School was out, he had his mother's present hidden in a shoebox, and Christmas was almost there. But later that morning, pouring out Jamie's soggy Cheerios from the yellow plastic bowl, Patty told him, "I was gonna try again to get to Littleton. You know, pick up a few presents." Then Jamie understood, and felt for her, because she wasn't ready for Christmas the way he was. "Well, we can't stay frozen in here forever," she said. "Not with all this sunshine."

Jamie knew they'd get out of the trailer. He could see, looking out the tiny window above the table, that the beautiful coating on the world was thin.

A little before noon they heard someone coming up the road. "Bet that's Earl," Patty said, hopping up to check, and it was. "Wouldn't you know?"

Jamie was always glad when it was Earl, and he clicked off the TV. A few seconds later, Earl was banging on the door. "You all in there?" he called out.

"Trapped," Patty called back, but her voice sounded like she was saying the opposite—that they were free as birds. "We thought we might have to live inside this ice cube forever," she continued, which wasn't even true, but Jamie knew that she was just making conversation. They could hear Earl chipping away at the ice. There had been so much buildup in one spot that

Earl had to take a propane torch to it. When he finally managed to budge the door open and step inside the trailer, the first thing he said was, "You're nuts, living out here."

"Yeah, well, we may be crazy, but you *look* crazy," Patty said. Earl was still holding the torch with its hissing blue flame, little ice crystals were clinging to his beard and mustache and eyelashes, and he had on his funny pointed cap with the flaps that came over his ears. Patty reached out and brushed some of the sparkles off his face. "Want coffee?"

Earl said what he'd really come for was to see his main man, Jamie. He told Jamie to get on his boots and grab his coat. "I'm delivering your present early," he told him. Patty started to say something, and Jamie and Earl both knew what it was going to be, but Earl cut her off at the pass. "Don't tell us we have to wait for Christmas, Pats," he said, "because today's the day. Right, Jamie?" (Jamie answered "Right" without missing a beat.) "You and Nin take the truck and go to Littleton. Just let me get Jamie's present."

Jamie could hardly believe how great things were going. He scrambled outside after Earl with his boots unclipped and his jacket unzipped. Earl was already reaching into the cab of his truck, and when he pulled back and faced Jamie he held up a tangle of ice skates, black leather and shiny silver blades, dangling in front of Jamie from their long, thick laces.

The sight of the skates sent a current through Jamie's body. He took off across the frozen ground toward the pond. He and Earl sat down on the rocks that ringed it, and pulled off their boots, and Earl untangled the skates and handed over Jamie's to him. They were heavy and clunky and awkward to put on. Jamie's hands were purple from the cold and he had a hard time making his fingers do what he wanted. Plus, he had holes in his socks and his big toes kept poking through. It was a struggle pulling the tongues of the skates straight and flat.

"Here," Earl said. "Let me give you a hand." He already had his skates tied, and he knelt down in front of Jamie, took the laces like little reins in his hands, and quickly threaded them through the holes. Jamie felt the skates securing themselves around him, becoming part of his feet, his ankles, bracing and stiff and strong, not like other things he'd worn.

Even before Earl had them tied, Jamie was scrambling to get up and take off, but no sooner was he up than he was back down again. "Hold on, buddy," Earl told him, and reached down and pulled him up by his wrists. Nothing felt familiar or right to Jamie. Eventually he got still, but even then Earl didn't take his hands away. They just stood there, face to face, for a while, not saying anything, not moving, as if getting steady was skating itself. Finally Earl said, "Ready?" and Jamie nodded, not really sure what he was agreeing to. Then Earl started moving backwards, making run-on S's with his skates and pulling Jamie forward with him. Jamie's feet started to splay out and Earl told him, "They're *your* feet. Pick 'em up when you need to."

It helped Jamie to remember his feet, their solidness, each and every toe. He lifted one foot and then the other, placed them down where he wanted them to be.

"Bend your knees a little," Earl told him. "Relax." The whole time he was holding on to Jamie's hands, leading him forward, gliding away from the edge of the pond. Jamie's impulse was to be scared, to clutch, to freeze, but little by little, following Earl's lead, lifting his feet up and taking short glides, he started to loosen up.

It was, for Jamie, a lot like when he'd learned to ride his bike. Right up until the moment the feeling went inside him, it was outside—in the bike, in his mother's hand on the seat, in the handlebars—somewhere, but not in him. And then, suddenly, *in* him.

That was happening now: the gliding was going inside him, into his legs and upper body and his arms and hands. He wasn't even holding Earl's hands anymore. Had he let go, or had Earl?

What had really gone inside him was a power: that's how it felt. He could make his body glide by pushing off one skate and then the other. He could go in a certain direction just by leaning that way. He could stop just by pulling back into himself. Even though some patches of the pond were so bumpy they made his teeth rattle when he skated over them and even though he nearly lost his balance when Earl skated by him going fast, and even though his hands were freezing, none of that stuff mattered. Being able to skate was all there was. There was nothing else in the world: nothing had happened before, nothing was coming up. There was just what he was doing, and how good it felt.

Jamie fell only once, and it was right at the very end, just as he approached the edge of the pond and was thinking about not skating, about getting the skates off and his boots back on. That's what tripped him up—thinking about going back to normal, walking, boots, ground. His skates came up from under him and he fell on his backside hard. It surprised him and hurt some, but mostly he was embarrassed. Jamie looked around quickly to see if anyone had seen him fall. Earl was making a fast ring around the pond, and when he got close to Jamie all he said was, "You did great."

10

Van showed up on Christmas Eve when Jamie was alone in the trailer with Nin. Patty had made a last-minute run to the store for a can of cranberries.

Jamie saw Van's truck coming down the road, saw it, knew who it was, and went and got Nin. He picked her up from her drawer and brought her into the bedroom. Without even thinking, he had a plan: he would hide under the bed—he'd crawl in first and then pull her in with him. But she was already squirming in his arms, close to waking up. And if she woke up, she'd cry, and he didn't want Van to hear her cry. That would be the worst thing.

So he laid her down on the far corner of his bed and yanked up the blankets and sheets into a little fortress around her. He did the best he could so no one would ever know she was there, and then dove under the bed alone and waited—the worst hide-and-seek he'd ever played.

He heard the knock, another knock, each as loud as his own hammering heart, and then he heard the door push open. "Patty?"

Jamie listened to Van step inside, and knew that once he was inside he could do anything he wanted: he could come looking, he could find Nin, he'd find her first.

Jamie pushed himself out from under the bed and into the bedroom, the daylight, the open. He checked the blankets around Nin again, then stepped out to keep Van from coming any closer.

As afraid as Jamie was, he was able to *see* Van: his real size, not larger than life, just this man in blue jeans and a work shirt and a thermal vest. He didn't look like he'd come to hurt anyone. Jamie thought Van looked scared himself.

"Hi, Van," Jamie said, his voice tight and dry.

Van gave him the quickest glance before he looked down. "Patty here?" he said. He took a drag on his cigarette.

"No," Jamie answered—started—but he didn't know how much to tell. Should he say that Patty had forgotten to get cranberries? Or that she was gone forever—moved to Texas, with Nin, and she was never coming back?

Van spoke first. "Okay if I wait for her?" he asked. At first Jamie didn't know what Van was talking about. Wait for her? For Patty? For what, and why was Van asking him, Jamie, as if Van ever asked Jamie if anything was all right to do? Jamie was utterly without answer, and when he didn't say anything, Van announced, "I'll wait outside."

Jamie ran back to the bedroom to look at Nin. She was sound asleep, not even close to crying, and nobody was going flying. Jamie tiptoed out of the room and looked out the little window above the kitchen table, at the road Patty would come driving up. He wanted her to come and he didn't want her to come.

Van stepped off the steps to the trailer and came into Jamie's field of vision. Jamie saw again that Van wasn't mad and he wasn't about to throw anything. He was there—where he didn't belong—but he was just there, smoking and kicking the icy ground with the heel of his boot, looking down.

Jamie went to the door, opened it, and said to Van, "I have a new magic trick. Wanna see?" Van could see Jamie's trick, and when Patty came home she could see Van's truck and turn around in a hurry, if she wanted to.

Van looked at Jamie, then dropped what was left of his cigarette onto the ice and crushed it under his boot. He walked back to the trailer and stepped inside.

Jamie had already set up the coin trick on the kitchen table. He would make nickels turn into dimes. "Here we have three nickels," he started, tapping the little ridged, silver-coin look-alikes with his black wand. It was the patter he had practiced so many times with Nin as his audience, in her little yellow rocking seat, as if all those hours of practice had been for this one moment with Van, this very moment.

His voice was dry and deadly serious.

"Three nickels as you can see." He was supposed to make eye contact with his audience, and he always did with Nin, but he skipped that part with Van and kept talking. "And I will turn these nickels into dimes before your very eyes." He heard a car, wheels on the road, and said louder, faster, "These nickels will become dimes before you know it." Van took a step toward the table to look out the window and see Patty's car coming down the road. Jamie tapped the pile again with his wand to get Van's attention. The car was still coming, it wasn't turning, the sound was louder, not fainter, and Van was watching it, not the trick.

"Three taps," Jamie continued, but no one was listening. He could have been speaking another language or none at all, he could've been talking in his sleep. Nin was still sleeping; that was good.

The car had stopped coming down the

road. Jamie gave up on the trick. He looked out then, too, to see if maybe Patty had turned around, even though he knew she hadn't, and saw instead her tearing toward the trailer, the car door open behind her.

She burst inside, wild. Just the sight of her, her enraged and terrified face, so terribly, totally there, scared Jamie, scared him more than Van had scared him.

There was a silent second when Van and Jamie stared at her and she stared back at them, and then Patty gasped, "Where's Nin?" Her drawer was empty, of course— Jamie had hidden her.

"She's here," Jamie said, as fast as he could, so she would know, wouldn't have to think something awful. "She's okay, she's here, she's sleeping," and he came out from behind the table to run and get her, to show his mother that Nin was all right, that he had protected her.

As Jamie walked by Patty, though, she grabbed his wrist and pulled him next to her, wrapped her arm around his shoulder. She was so strong. "She's okay?" she repeated and Jamie nodded at her, and Patty just tightened her grip around his shoulder and said, "Good boy."

So Jamie and Patty stood side by side and faced Van, who hadn't said or done anything since Patty had burst into the trailer.

"What do you want?" she said to Van. "What are you doing here?"

Again Jamie looked at Van and saw him as he had first seen him: skinny, stooped, nervous, but as drained as he'd been after he threw the baby, threw Nin. Van was done. He wasn't scary. Patty had been scary, but she wasn't anymore. She was beside Jamie, her arm around him.

Van shuffled and managed to raise his

eyes only slightly for the briefest look at Patty. "Can I talk to you a minute?"

There was a cry from the bedroom. A little short cry and then nothing, and then a series of sounds—little cries, jabbering. Patty's hand tightened on Jamie's shoulder and then released. "Go get her, Jamie," she said. "Get her and take her outside and start walking toward school and I'll come and get you after I talk to Van for a second."

Jamie looked at his mother.

"Do it," she said.

He turned and went into the bedroom. Nin was rolled over in the mound of blankets he had bunched up around her, pulling at the striped design on the blanket.

"Hello, baby," he said—heard himself say—"hello, baby," nice and easy and gentle, the way his mother did, so Nin could wake up slowly and not get all rattled and crabby. He leaned down over her and she smiled up at him, kicked her legs in anticipation of being lifted up. Suddenly what his mother had told him to do next—to take Nin and walk down the road, to leave—came over him and he couldn't stand it.

He turned and walked out of the room without Nin. Van and his mother hadn't moved an inch. "No," he said. He wouldn't go away from the trailer and his mother, wouldn't leave her, wouldn't take care of Nin one more second. "No," he said again, as if he had the power to send back a wave. He looked at his mother and she looked at him, and everything he was feeling traveled between them, on some invisible cable that connected their hearts.

Patty finally nodded, and no sooner was the matter settled, without a word, than Van broke the silence and surprised them all by saying, "I'll go." Patty and Jamie both looked at him. "I'll go," he said again.

Even with everything that was going on inside him—or maybe because of it—Jamie felt for Van. It was so obvious no one wanted him: the same as not getting picked for the team. Part of Jamie even wanted to say, "No, no, you can stay," but it wasn't a strong enough part to have its own voice, so he didn't say anything at all.

Van stepped to the door and then said to Jamie's mother, "I'll come around some other time."

Jamie looked at his feet, his sneakers, held his breath, and heard his mother say, "No." It wasn't her mean voice, but she did say it: "No. Don't you do that. Don't come around."

Jamie kept watching his sneakers, listened to the moment of silence, then the door opening, then the slam.

All he could think to do was go get Nin. He couldn't look at his mother yet, couldn't raise his eyelids that high. So he got Nin and put her in her yellow rocker on the kitchen table and rocked her.

His mother hadn't said a word either. She'd walked over to the sink, started the water running, and squirted some soap into the plastic bucket. She was moving fast, the way she sometimes did, and when she grabbed a dirty plate to wash, she accidentally smacked it up against the faucet.

The crack might as well have gone through Jamie's backbone, as if he were the plate, snapped in half. He burst into tears that came with such force it was all he could do to keep standing. His crying was way beyond being a baby and way beyond being dangerous—the only two things he'd known about crying up until that moment. He cried and cried and cried, huge air-gobbling sobs that he could feel in his back and that he couldn't stop, even when Patty was kneeling down and had her arms around him, saying, "It's all right, oh it's all right, sweetie, it's okay, we're okay."

Jamie buried his face in the soft darkness of his mother's sweatshirt and cried some more, until finally whatever needed to be out of him was. Then he drew in stuttery breaths and the pounding in his chest began to slow. He wiped his cheeks with the backs of his hands and they were so wet, so covered with tears, that he felt like he had washed his face.

Jamie had cried himself out and was done, but Nin had started and was going strong. When Jamie and Patty finally turned to her, she was rigid with outrage in her little yellow seat. They couldn't help laughing at how she looked—her scrunched crimson face and arched back, how furious she was at being ignored. Patty lifted her out of her rocker and said, "Oh, you're all right, too, miss baby. You're all right, too," and rocked her from side to side. It didn't take long to quiet her, and when she had, Patty caught Jamie's eye and they both laughed again, the way people do who have been through something together.

"Get her a juice bottle," Patty said, and Jamie went to the refrigerator and grabbed one.

"Here," he said, handing it over.

Patty settled down with Nin in the easy chair. "How about some magic?" she asked.

Yes. That was just what Jamie wanted, too. He took all the time he needed, and then Jamie began.